Hausaland Tales

from the Nigerian Marketplace

Hausaland Tales
from the
Nigerian Marketplace

by
Gavin McIntosh

Linnet Books
North Haven, Connecticut

Library of Congress Cataloging-in-Publication-Data

McIntosh, Gavin, 1953-
    Hausaland tales from the Nigerian marketplace / by Gavin McIntosh.
        p. cm.
    Summary: A collection of twelve traditional tales from the Hausa people of
Nigeria.
    ISBN 0-208-02523-5 (alk. paper)
        1. Hausa (African people)—Folklore. 2. Tales—Nigeria. [1. Hausa (African
people)—Folklore. 2. Nigeria—Folklore.] I. Title.
PZ8.1.M184 Hau 2002
398.2'089'937—dc21

                                                                    2002022603

The paper in this publication meets the minimum requirements
of American National Standard for Information Sciences—
Permanence of Paper for Printed Library Materials,
ANSI Z39.48—1984.∞

All photographs appearing in this book were taken by Gavin McIntosh.

Designed by Carol Sawyer of Rose Design

Printed in the United States of America

To Robbie and Breanna
who began life as this book took form.

Contents

Acknowledgments

I would like to acknowledge the hospitality and generosity of the many other CUSO volunteers who helped me collect the folktales in this book. I also wish to acknowledge the work of Ibrahim Madauci, Yahaya Isa, and Bello Daura, *Hausa Customs,* published by The Northern Nigerian Publishing Company Ltd., P.O. Box 412, Zaria, Sokoto State, 1968, which was used to check many of the facts in this book.

An Impression of Hausaland

For a thousand years the Hausa people have been traders in sub-Saharan Africa. The ancient trade routes of the eleventh century have gradually developed into a trading network that connects Hausaland to cities as far away as Cairo and Dakar. Hausaland is the name of the region inhabited primarily by the Hausa people. It stretches from parts of the West African countries of Benin in the east, Niger in the north, Nigeria in the south, to Cameroon in the east. Approximately 20 million people speak the language of Hausa as their mother tongue.

There are two main seasons in Hausaland. The rainy season begins in June and continues to September. In the rainy season, torrential rains allow a growing season for crops such as yams, guinea corn, and cassava. The dry season extends from October until April. It is also referred to as the hot season. The heat in sub-Saharan Africa, with an average year-round temperature of 85 degrees F (32 degrees C), can be oppressive. During times of drought, widespread economic hardship can prevail throughout Hausaland. Though it includes areas of jungle, savannah, and even mountainous highlands, throughout much of Hausaland the landscape stretches, flat and parched in all directions. Sand blown across the dry, brown fields by the fierce *harmattan* winds collects in drifts against the walls of mud-bricked houses. Even

in this predominately hot, dry climate most Hausa people living in rural areas have maintained their traditional pastoral life where the family grows a small vegetable garden and many raise goats, chickens, cattle, or even camels.

Hausa people cohabit the region with many other ethnic groups as well. For instance, many Fulani people live in the northern range of the Hausa people. Yoruba people from the south also live in Hausaland. The Dogon people from Mali, well-known for their ceremonial costumes and wooden masks, also live among the Hausa in Cameroon. In Nigeria alone there are some 300 ethnic groups, all with their own languages, dialects, and customs. Often there are significant differences between the customs of one village and the next. However, in Hausaland almost all Hausa people practice the religion of Islam. As Muslims, they follow strict Islamic religious practices. The beliefs or practices of the characters in the folktales in this book, however, do not reflect those of the Muslim people or of other modern Nigerians, and should not be confused with them by the reader.

For two years, from 1981 to 1983, I worked and lived at a government secondary school in the rural town of Gwadabawa, Sokoto State, Nigeria, in the heart of Hausaland. I went to Nigeria to work with eighty other CUSO volunteers. CUSO is a Canadian organization dedicated to helping in developing countries around the world, very similar to the Peace Corps in the United States. Most of us were assigned teaching jobs in rural schools. An oil boom in the 1970s had brought a period of prosperity to Nigeria. The government was able to introduce a system called Universal Primary Education. This initiative had reached its peak when I arrived in Nigeria. Because of the new education policies, many boys and girls from remote areas of Nigeria were given financial allowances for transportation, food, and supplies to attend regional boarding schools. Often these students were the first members of their family to attend school and receive a formal education. By the end of 1983, the boom was finished and a military government had taken over. Military governments have been in place for most of the time. The period of time when I worked in Nigeria was fairly unique. As it turned out, it was an ideal time to collect folktales.

Facilities at our school were very basic. Electricity was rarely available. Water for school meals and washing had to be carried from town wells by the students each morning in buckets on their heads. Organized entertainment was virtually nonexistent, and students were left to devise their own amusement. The students at G.S.S. Gwadabawa loved to tell each other stories from their hometowns. Their versions of the stories were often enriched for effect with a good measure of personal embellishment. The best storytellers enjoyed high status at the school.

After hearing some amazing folktales, and having heard different versions of the same stories originating in different towns, I asked friends teaching in other towns to look for individuals who knew other folktales. In those days I drove a little Honda 125 motorcycle. On it I was able to travel the day's journey to visit other schools and hear more folktales from the students there. By hearing the same folktales from different sources I was able to verify that certain ones were indigenous to the region. The memory of traveling through the countryside, along dusty roads and open fields, is one of my most treasured of those days.

In Hausaland, village life revolves around the weekly market days when everyone gets together at the central marketplace to practice local crafts such as grass mat weaving and leather work, and sell food and household goods. Early on market day the road is teeming with people walking or riding to market. Trucks rumble by with dozens of people clinging to the sides or tops. Men and women walk proudly along with several items balanced effortlessly on their heads.

Children cluster around each newcomer to offer eggs, salt, or plastic bags for sale.

The marketplace can be a bewildering mixture of sights, sounds, and smells which combine to produce something part-commerce and part-circus. A maze of pathways is created around the vendors who display their wares on brightly colored cloths. Traders bring a wide variety of things from near and far. The scene is filled with lively joking and arguing as the exchange of local news and gossip is shouted back and forth.

At night, vendors set up small wooden tables along the town streets. Hundreds of kerosene bush lamps glow like flickering starlight. It seems as though everyone in town must be selling something. The pace is relaxed, a time for entertaining and visiting with neighbors.

Sometimes at the marketplace one of the elders will share a tale about something that may or may not have happened long ago. In Hausaland, the people have traditionally relied on Hausa, an oral language, to organize their complex culture, and storytelling has developed to bring people together and share their ideas and values. Parents pass on their versions of folktales to their children, and so it goes.

In *Hausaland Tales from the Nigerian Marketplace,* the marketplace scenes preceding each folktale are intended to provide a social context to illustrate how folktales are a part of daily life and evolve from the teller's experiences. I have set all Hausa words in italics and they are in the glossary. Other words defined in the glossary are italicized for their first appearance in any story. The characters in the marketplace scenes are fictitious, but do represent individuals I met at the Gwadabawa *kasuwa* on market day. Electricity at my house was usually not working, and so of course there was no refrigeration. I shopped at our local marketplace in Gwadabawa without fail, and it was the highlight of my week.

No matter whether the Hausa people I met were young or old, or from rural or urban areas, they loved to hear of North America and especially New York City. While I shared some folktales from my own childhood, it was usually the "glamor" of Western life that appealed to them. I guess I did not think of North America as being all that glamorous, because I was always more interested in hearing their folktales. When you read these stories from Hausaland maybe you'll see why I like them best.

U maru the weaver walked along the road with several carefully folded bundles of cloth balanced high on his head. He stepped to the side to let a honking motorcycle pass. The red dust of the desert was everywhere. The dry *harmattan* winds had only recently subsided, but already the hot season was beginning. Even in the early morning the heat seemed to hang over everything like a blanket. Herds of wandering goats continued to consume anything remotely edible near the ground. Only the *nim* trees, with their roots deep in the earth, seemed to defy the heat and flourish. Their long, narrow leaves and crimson berries brightened the roadside and cast welcome shade on the procession.

The familiar clip-clop of a trotting donkey came up beside Umaru. On its rump sat Musa the potter. A large straw *Fulani* hat covered his head. His pots were wrapped in burlap and strung across the withers of the donkey.

"*Sannu, ina kwana?*" called Musa in greeting. "How did you sleep?"

"*Lafiya lau,*" replied Umaru. "Fine."

1

"*Ina aiki?*" asked Musa. "How is work?"

"*Aiki da godia,*" said Umaru. "Work is good, thanks be to God."

"You seem unusually happy today, Umaru. Have you brought many robes to sell?" said Musa.

"Even better. I have a story to tell today that will amaze everyone, even Bello the leather worker," chuckled Umaru.

"So tell me now. We still have a long way to go to the marketplace," said Musa.

"Okay, but if I do, you have to tell a story of your own after that," replied Umaru.

"How do you know I have a story today?" countered Musa.

"You always have a story. But never the five *naira* you owe me!" laughed Umaru.

"And you always have a complaint, old man," laughed Musa. "All right, go ahead, I'm listening."

And so, Umaru began his story.

Why the Red-Necked Lizard Nods His Head

If you have ever watched a red-necked lizard you will have seen a strange sight. It is the habit of this nervous creature to run a few steps, stop, and then violently jerk its head up and down. Here is the story of how this curious behavior began.

A long time ago there was a king who had two beautiful daughters. He decided that they would both marry the same suitor, but that the lucky groom must also be the cleverest in the kingdom.

The two girls had always been kept away from other people. They only moved about in their rooms and in the lovely garden within their compound. No one except the royal family knew their names.

The king decided that only the wisest of his subjects would be able to discover the names of his daughters. So he sent out a proclamation that whoever could tell him the names of his daughters would marry them and be given a palace of his own as well.

In the kingdom lived a poor but extremely clever tortoise. When he heard of the king's generous offer he sat down and thought for a long time. Then he went to the garden where the girls strolled each afternoon.

The garden was surrounded by a tall, smooth wall that no one could ever climb. Tortoise could hear the princesses playing in the courtyard. Beside the wall grew a large, spreading mango tree. Tortoise studied the tree for a long time. He could see that one tree branch grew high above and over the wall.

Tortoise was not a good climber. With his short, stubby legs and heavy shell on his back it took all his strength to gradually haul himself up the tree trunk and onto the branch. Eventually he managed to crawl along the branch until he was looking down into the courtyard. Concealed among the leaves and fruit, he could safely spy on the girls below him. They were the most beautiful girls he had ever seen.

As he hid beside the mango fruit, Tortoise had an idea how he might lure the girls close enough so that he could hear what they were saying. He picked a juicy, ripe mango and carefully tossed it so he could see where it dropped. The soft, mushy fruit hit the ground, "SSSSPLAT!" and exploded in all directions. One of the girls came over to see what had made the noise. Tortoise was enchanted by her beauty. He could not help offering another ripe mango. He let it drop right at her feet.

"SSSPLAT!" went the second soft, mushy mango. "Oh no, Huseina! I have mango all over my dress!" she cried.

The delighted tortoise now knew the name of one of the princesses. Huseina came over to look. She was as beautiful as the first girl, and Tortoise dropped another mango for her.

"SSSSPLAT!" went the third soft, mushy mango.

"Oh no, Hasana. Now I have mango all over my dress too!"

Tortoise was overjoyed. Now he knew both the names of the princesses, but he had to escape before he was discovered!

"What is that in the tree?" cried Huseina.

"It is crawling away!" shouted Hasana. They began throwing mango pits at the unfortunate Tortoise. They were both expert throwers.

"ZING!" One pit sailed over Tortoise's head as he crawled back into the mango leaves.

"ZING!" Another one whistled past his ear, as he hurried back along the branch.

"ZING! ZING!" Two more came at once and hit the rear end of Tortoise's shell just as he headed down the slippery tree trunk.

Tortoise fell head over heels down the trunk and landed on the ground with a loud "WUMPH." Tortoise was able to limp away, but his shell was cracked into many pieces. To this day you can see the pattern of the cracks on Tortoise's shell.

After the terrible fall Tortoise felt dazed. How could he remember the names of the two princesses? Tortoise kept repeating the names so that he would not forget them. "Huseina, Huzoona—no. Huseina, Hasana, Huseina, Hasana . . . peel me a banana! Huseina, Hasana . . . Huseina, Hasana, peel me a banana," he mumbled as he limped all the way around the palace to the front gates. The gates were huge with bars running from top to bottom. At one side stood a small gatehouse for the king's messenger. Armed with the secret knowledge of the names, Tortoise knocked boldly at the gate. The king's messenger, an ugly brown lizard, answered.

Tortoise announced, "Tell the king I have come to marry his daughters. Their names are . . . their names are . . . their names are Huseina, Hasana, peel me a banana!"

The surprised messenger quickly peeled Tortoise a banana and ran for the king. On the way he thought about marrying the beautiful princesses and living in the palace. When he approached the king he claimed, "Sire, I know the names of your daughters. In a dream I heard the names Huseina and Hasana."

The king was greatly troubled. He knew Lizard well and could not believe that this was the cleverest of his subjects. Yet the king felt obliged to keep his word, and made arrangements for the royal wedding.

Tortoise was left standing at the gates. After a very long time Tortoise pushed his head through the bars to look for Lizard. He could barely turn his head to see, but he could hear a great commotion coming from inside the palace. Eventually, he heard the news of Lizard's forthcoming marriage. He was furious and solemnly vowed to avenge himself.

However, when Tortoise tried to pull his head back he found it was stuck. Again and again he pulled. His little ears were pinned against the sides of his head. With every pull he stretched his neck until it felt as though it would snap in two. Finally, with a desperate tug, Tortoise fell back. He did not have far to fall because his neck had stretched to twice its length. He was free, but when he checked the painful sides of his head he found that his ears had been rubbed right off! Even to this day Tortoise has a long neck and no ears sticking out of his head, and if you try to touch his head he is quick to pull it back into his shell.

Throughout Tortoise's ordeal he had been watched by the king's prized white rooster, which perched on the gatehouse. It was one of the king's most treasured possessions and it was the responsibility of the king's messenger, Lizard, to look after it. Now the rooster tilted its head and fixed Tortoise with a beady yellow eye. It clucked and crowed a laugh of scorn down on Tortoise's misfortune. This enraged Tortoise, who snatched the bird from its roost. Though it squawked loudly enough for all to hear, Tortoise put it under his arm and hurried home with it. Quickly he killed, boiled, and ate the rooster.

While the king's guards were searching throughout the palace for the missing bird, Tortoise carried the boiling water and the rooster's remains to Lizard's gatehouse. He threw the feathers and bones all over the floor. Lizard was terrified.

The guards' footsteps drew nearer the gatehouse. Tortoise leaned close to the cowering Lizard and threatened, "Drink every last drop of this magic potion or you will surely suffer. It can make you invisible." He handed the bowl of water to Lizard through the bars.

Without a thought, Lizard gulped down the scalding liquid. It was so hot that he spit out violently—"AAAUK PHOOTSU"—onto Tortoise's head. All of Tortoise's hair curled up and broke off. Now he was completely bald, and he has remained bald ever since. Lizard's throat was so badly burned that it turned bright, bright red and he lost his voice. All he could do was jerk his head up and down to cool his throat. And this he did. Up and down. Up and down. Up and down!

The king's guards stormed into the gatehouse and saw the bones and white feathers on the floor. Immediately Lizard and Tortoise were dragged to the king's throne room.

The king accused Lizard, "Is it true that you ate my royal rooster?" Lizard's throat was on fire. He rapidly bobbed his head up and down. *"Kai,"* said the king as he noted Lizard's confession.

The king turned to Tortoise. "And what do you have to say for yourself?"

Tortoise tried to remember the names of the princesses. But his head already hurt and remembering seemed to make it hurt even more. Then suddenly it came to him and he blurted out, "Huseina, Hasana . . . Huseina, Hasana, peel me a banana."

"Tortoise, I am delighted to hear you say that. If you know the names of my daughters, then you are the one to marry them." The king was very relieved that Lizard had not won his contest. Tortoise told the king how he had discovered the names of the princesses and about Lizard's trick.

"Kai! Kai! Lizard, did you deceive me in this manner?" the king demanded. Lizard again nodded his head.

"Kai! Kai! Kai! Do you think I am a fool?" the king raged. Lizard nodded his head for the last time. The king

ordered that the evil lizard be removed and his hyperactive head be chopped off.

There was a grand wedding held that day with Tortoise marrying the two beautiful princesses. Both the princesses thought Tortoise looked very handsome with all his new features. They never threw mango pits at him again and were happy to peel him bananas. They all lived happily together from that day on in a splendid palace of their own. And from that day to this, all the lizards in the kingdom have red necks and nod their heads.

—Based on a story told by Mohammed Adamu

Maganin maki gudu ban kashi.
Desperate times call for desperate measures.

"Ha! Is that the best story you have?" teased Musa. "I have a better one than that. And why not? In my family, the knowledge of pottery making has been passed down from father to son for six generations. And with it has come wonderful stories of long ago." The potter leaned forward and tapped a beautiful small-necked *shantali* water pot. "You know, to fire a pot properly without a kiln takes great skill. The sticks for the fire must be stacked around the pot to exactly the correct thickness or the pot will crack. Our craft took centuries to perfect."

As the two men approached the mud-brown waters of the Tazarawa River, a lone Tuareg rider mounted on a huge tawny camel crossed the road in front of them. Tuaregs are a nomadic people who live throughout the Sahara Desert. For centuries they have linked oasis towns with cities around the desert, transporting salt on their camels to exchange for millet, sugar, tea, and cloth. The Tuaregs once dominated most trade routes across the desert and taxed its caravans. In more recent times, some Tuaregs had taken jobs in Hausaland, often working as guards. They had the reputation of being fearless.

The gigantic camel towered above everyone. Musa's donkey suddenly veered away, causing all the pots to clack against one another. The Tuareg rider was dressed from head to foot in black. Only his eyes were visible as he passed by and continued down the sloped bank to a flat, sandy boat landing by the river. Cold and confident, his eyes seemed amused by the little donkey heavily laden with pots of all shapes and old Musa, all but hidden among them. With the rolling gait of the camel, the mysterious man's black robes flowed behind like cascading sand dunes. The long sword strapped to his waist seemed well-used.

Perhaps the Tuareg was guarding other camels, for there were thirty or forty of the one-humped dromedaries down at the riverbank. The camels were being washed by several boys, wearing shorts and flip-flop sandals. Some of the great beasts drank with lowered heads as the boys scrubbed them with brushes and poured water from buckets over their long legs.

Once the camel was safely behind them, the donkey snorted its disapproval and surged ahead. Musa seemed lost in thought for a moment, as he reined in the donkey and waited for Umaru to catch up.

"Well, I hope it won't take centuries for you to get to the story," urged Umaru.

"Never fear, my friend. From my father's father, to my father, to me, to you, I say the best type of clay to make these pots comes only from the edge of the riverbed. And along the river are strange sights you could never dream of here. I have been to the deserts of the north and the jungles in the south and I have heard one story that might make even you smile," Musa began.

The Race

Once long ago, there was a race among the river folk to see who was the fastest among them. The race was a strange one and the story of the race has been repeated time after time from then until now. This is how it happened.

For some time, Frog had been disturbed by a problem. Her large family lived along the riverbank among the reeds and grasses. Life was pleasant enough for them, except that Hippopotamus took no notice of frogs. She tramped through the marsh as if the frogs were not there, "PUCOO, PUCOO, PUCOO," and crushed many of them under her great weight.

Wherever Hippo went, she was accompanied by two attendants. A small, yellow-billed oxpecker perched on her back and pecked at insects behind her ears. Amid the preening, Oxpecker continually praised Hippo, singing songs about all the great deeds that Hippo had done in her life. Behind Hippo stalked a stately egret, whose spindly legs carried him above the grass and whose long, deadly beak was equally quick to spear insects or frogs, which were scattered by Hippo's footsteps.

Now, it was acknowledged by all the river folk that Hippo was the fastest runner among them—maybe the fastest in the whole world! So one day, Frog decided that if she could win a race against Hippo, then finally the frogs might win respect and be left in peace.

Frog asked Lion, King of the Beasts, to call a meeting of all the animals. When they were gathered together, Frog stood up and boldly challenged Hippo to a race. Hippo only snorted "KUHOO" at the tiny frog's audacity, but a date was set for the contest.

A long course was marked out on the path, which lay beside the winding river. Three resting spots were chosen in case the runners became too tired. As the day for the race approached, Hippo spent her time demonstrating her speed by thrashing back and forth in front of a group of wide-eyed spectators. Oxpecker called out to the crowd that no one could beat Hippo because Hippo was unbeatable. Egret eyed the crowd, ready to spear anyone who disagreed. Oxpecker sang:

Run Hippo Run
HIPPO HIPPO HIPPO
Run Hippo Run
HIPPO HIPPO HIPPO

Frog sat at a safe distance and perfected her plan. Frog knew that great beasts like Hippo never bothered to look closely at smaller animals such as frogs. There are subtle differences between all creatures, and Frog had no trouble telling the difference between her children. However, she knew that to Hippo all frogs looked exactly the same.

When the sun rose on the morning of the race, Frog was already at work with four of her children. She left one of them at the starting point. The other three were given instructions and dropped off at the three resting places along the course. Frog herself hid near the finish line.

When Hippo arrived at the appointed time, there was a frog waiting for her. Lion roared "GRRAAARR" to start the race. The crowd cheered as Hippo rushed into a quick lead. But to her surprise, as she approached the first resting place, there was Frog just hopping away, "PLIP, PLIP, PLIP." Hippo did not stop, and soon outdistanced her opponent. Egret was beginning to tire and even his long legs could not keep up the pace. Oxpecker hung onto Hippo's ear as she was bounced back and forth, "BLOMP, FLOP, BLOMP, FLOP."

At the next rest stop Hippo could not believe her eyes. Again Frog was in front! With a bellow, Hippo ignored the second resting place and thundered past, "PUCOO, PUCOO, PUCOO." Now Egret was tired and discouraged by how the race was going. When Hippo ran on, Egret stayed behind. Oxpecker continued to hang on, but saw that Egret was no longer with them.

By the time she reached the third rest stop, Hippo was exhausted. The scorching sun beat down on her broad back, stealing the last of her strength. And yet there ahead of her, as fresh as ever, was Frog going "PLIP, PLIP, PLIP." Hippo refused to stop and lumbered on. Oxpecker finally let go of Hippo's ear and flew away to find a safer roost.

In a feverish rage, Hippo lunged towards the finish line. But as she came within sight of it, there was Frog jumping lightly across to win the race! Hippo made a ridiculous sight as she weaved and heaved in front of the crowd. Everyone laughed and made fun of her. There was no attendant now to follow or to praise her. Frog was declared the winner of the race! Now the river folk sang:

> Hop Frog Hop
> FROG FROG FROG
> Hop Frog Hop
> FROG FROG FROG

The disgraced Hippo staggered away and was never seen again. From that day on, Frog and her family lived in peace by the river.

—*Based on a story told by Abubakar Idris*

Abin da zuciya ta dauka gangar jiki bawa ne.
Where there is a will there is a way.

To someone seeing the market-place for the first time it might appear a chaotic jumble of vendors surrounded by a throng of customers. But this is far from true. Actually the market is divided into many sections. The food vendors all sit in a certain area, the clothing vendors in another spot. The meat sellers have their own section, and so on. This organization helps people familiar with the market to easily find what they want.

But there is also a special spot near the center of the market. It is here that Umaru and Musa always set up. At this spot the boundaries of several different categories of vendors converge. The vendors at this location sell different things, but they all have something in common. They love to hear and to tell stories. They are all superb storytellers and they love to entertain each other with their treasures. For this group, market day always passes too quickly, and they can't wait to return in seven days to share new stories gathered during the week.

Umaru and Musa approached the blacksmith who sat hunched over his hot coals of *kirya* wood. He was using

goatskin bellows to pump air onto the white-hot coals. The heat shimmered up in waves. Umaru announced in a loud voice, "Well, we might as well sit here. Ibrahim the blacksmith won't be needing this space for customers!"

"*Kai!* You know you just want to watch me at work to learn how to do a real trade," said the blacksmith. He squinted and shielded his face from the heat as he smiled at his friends. His tongs gripped the long, pointed *modoshi* rod, which he pulled out of the fire and used to burn a hole into the head of a short-handled *garma* hoe. He held out the handle at arm's length to display it.

"I know a *groundnut* farmer who will be happy to pay me a sack of nuts for this hoe. Now, I don't mind waiting for the harvest to be paid. I am used to waiting. In fact, I have been saving this spot, waiting here for hours for you two lazy merchants to arrive. Listen to this story and you will see how hard-working and patient someone must be to get the groundnuts he deserves!" Ibrahim smiled, for he knew that this was a story his friends would like.

Why Vulture Has a Bare Neck

Once, long ago, Vulture lived in the bush with other animals. Vulture was not afraid of anyone and boasted all the time that he could see farther than anyone. He rarely did any work, but always kept a keen eye out for any opportunity for a free meal. In those days Vulture's favorite food was *groundnuts,* which some people call peanuts. There were many groundnut farms in the area and that meant many delicious temptations for Vulture.

In the middle of the groundnut country lived *Grasscutter.* Grasscutter was a large, hard-working rodent and a very successful groundnut farmer. His farm was the pride of his life. He even lived in a burrow among the roots of his groundnut bushes.

Every few days Vulture would fly in circles above the farm. When he was sure no one was watching he would swoop down and steal some groundnuts. Then he would boast about how clever he was to always find groundnuts without the bother of farming.

By the end of the harvest season there were no groundnuts left except those stored in Grasscutter's house. One night, Vulture entered the house and refused to leave. He cocked his ugly head to one side and spread his long straggly wings wide and said, "Listen to me. I live here and here I will stay." Grasscutter had little choice but to leave or be eaten along with the groundnuts.

Now, it happened that Grasscutter's house actually belonged to Warthog. Years before, Warthog and Grasscutter had reached a friendly agreement and Grasscutter was allowed to use the burrow for as long as he liked. Hearing of Grasscutter's unfortunate situation, Warthog came back to claim his house.

Vulture refused to move. He cocked his ugly head to one side and spread his long, straggly wings out wide and said, "Listen to me. I live here and here I will stay."

"But the burrow really belongs to me. I own it," complained Warthog.

"Ha! Where is your agreement in writing? Where are your witnesses? If you can't prove otherwise, the farm, the groundnut bushes, the burrow and especially the delicious groundnuts are mine!"

There was nothing for Warthog to do but go home. Vulture enjoyed his fortune to the fullest, living comfortably on Grasscutter's supply of groundnuts.

The only neighbor who enjoyed the company of Vulture was Hyena. Hyena laughed at anything and he thought Vulture's greed was amusing. Hyena often invited Vulture to supper. Neither animal ever left a meal while there was anything remaining to eat. And they always washed down their food with kegs of palm wine.

One night Hyena ate and drank until his belly sagged and his legs could barely carry him. Hyena's head was spinning from drinking all the palm wine. He laughed and laughed. He said that Vulture was his best friend, a fine fellow, and whatever he had was Vulture's to take. Then Hyena fell asleep. Vulture saw this as a wonderful opportunity. That very night when he left Hyena's house he took with him all of Hyena's groundnuts.

The following morning the silly Hyena woke up and could not remember a thing except that Vulture had visited for supper the night before. When he discovered that all his groundnuts were gone, he raised a terrible cry. Soon a large crowd of animals had gathered in front of his house. As soon as they learned the cause of Hyena's wailing, they all marched to Vulture's house. There they found Vulture with the groundnuts, loudly protesting his innocence.

Vulture cocked his ugly head to one side and spread his long, straggly wings out wide. "Listen to me. Didn't you tell me that what was yours was mine?" he cried.

"I do not remember anything like that," Hyena replied truthfully.

Angry murmurs traveled through the crowd. Many in the crowd were from Grasscutter's growing family. "Stealing is a serious crime!" they shouted. Unfortunately, Hyena could not help laughing, and this made everyone even angrier.

Then from the back of the crowd, Warthog's voice called out, "You say those groundnuts are yours. Where is your agreement in writing? Where are your witnesses?"

The animals went wild. They tried to punish the giggling Hyena for his insolence, but he ran away with his tail between his legs. Then they grabbed Vulture and tied a rope around his feet and his neck and hung him over the groundnut bushes. As Vulture thrashed about, he cocked his head to one side and he spread out his wings. "Listen to me!" he cried. But no one did.

The rope rubbed all the feathers off Vulture's neck before it finally slipped over his narrow head and he was able to hop quickly away. To this day the feathers have never grown back on his ugly, bare neck.

Vulture and Hyena were banished from the groundnut farm. Now both have to scavenge their meals from wherever they can find them. Vulture still swoops down for a free meal whenever he can, but he quickly hops away when others approach because he is afraid of another beating.

—*Based on a story told by Nuhu Mutala*

Kowa ya zubar mani da tsamiyata sai
in zubar masa da nononsa.
Pay back in the same coin.

The group was joined by Amina, the lovely young vegetable seller. Her slender form moved through the market with ease. In both hands Amina carried bowls stacked with piles of tomatoes like little pyramids. On her head she balanced a woven basket of groundnuts. A brightly colored groundcloth was tucked under her arm. As Amina sat down on her cloth, silver bracelets slid down her arm with a musical clatter.

"Of course everyone wants groundnuts. I could hear you all the way across the field, Ibrahim. Groundnuts are delicious and cheap, too. You will have enough money left over to buy some fine *gari* meal!" she called in a voice heard by all.

"Be careful where you walk, woman. Can't you see we are trying to play a game of *Dara?*" snapped Umaru.

Umaru the weaver had dug out two rows of six shallow *Dara* hollows in the ground. At both ends of the rows were two bigger hollows. Musa was smiling as he scooped some smooth polished stones from one of the hollows. "Thank

22

you, Umaru! You never have to try to bring pleasure to your
opponents," Musa said.

Amina ignored Umaru. She turned to Musa saying,
"Potter, why don't you make your own style of *Dara* stones
from clay? You know, people play this game now everywhere. They call it *Mancala*. You could add some color to
the game."

"Why should I care? I already have these stones and they
are more than good enough to beat Umaru every time!"
joked Musa.

Umaru looked up from the *Dara* game long enough to
scowl at Amina and mutter, "How can I concentrate with all
this monkey-chatter in my ear?" Amina just looked from

Umaru to Musa and then to Ibrahim and Bello the leather worker. She shook her head and laughed, "Oh no, stay away from this one! He is dangerous today!"

"My advice to all of you is to stay away from Amina's millet cakes," cautioned Ibrahim to the group sitting around him. "Last week I bit down on a stone in one that almost broke my jaw," he moaned.

"You should have used your *masaba* hammer on the cakes first. Isn't that how you make *gari* mash with Amina's *cassava?*" laughed Bello.

"Ha, very funny! Laugh all you want, Bello. Food is the life of the village. When the crops fail there is no money for anyone to buy your leather. After you hear my story you will thank me for my *gari* meal and millet cakes," said Amina as she began her story.

The Leopard
and the Rat

In the spreading branches of a guava tree lived a mean, old leopard. Among the roots of the great tree was a hole and in the hole lived a skinny rat. Rat was so undernourished because Leopard took most of her food. In fact, Leopard rarely bothered to hunt at all. Instead, he forced Rat to scour the countryside and bring him any food she could find.

Rat knew that if she refused, it would not be long before Leopard caught and ate her. The only thing that sustained Rat was the occasional guava fruit that fell from the tree. Eventually there came a day when there was no food to be found anywhere. Rat was terrified at the prospect of failing to satisfy Leopard's usual demand.

At the last minute Rat thought of a place she had seen on one of her long forays. It was a village of humans where much food was kept. Rat begged Leopard to be patient and to postpone his meal until dark when they might slip into the village unnoticed.

When they arrived at the village all was quiet. They walked among the houses where people slept. Rat and Leopard moved soundlessly through the winding streets until they came to a huge larder of food at the center of the village. The door to the larder was made of stout poles lashed together at the ends. Rat set to work on the cords, "NITS, NITS, NITS," and soon had one pole cut free. There was just enough room for Rat and Leopard to squeeze through.

Inside, millet cakes were stacked on metal shelves from floor to ceiling. Leopard set about devouring all the millet cakes. Leopard ate all night until, just before sunrise, almost all the food was gone. Though Rat was starving and her skin hung on her bones like a thin blanket, Leopard would not let her touch a crumb.

At last Leopard could eat no more. His swollen belly fairly dragged on the floor. Yet, when Rat reached for the last millet cake, the mean leopard could not bear to let her have it. Instead, he swiped with his powerful paw and sent the cake flying across the room. Leopard turned to leave, but now he was too fat—"NUUUH, OOOU, UH"—to fit through the opening in the door!

Frustrated and furious, Leopard looked around for another exit and saw that there was none. Anger surged in Leopard as he looked around again—this time for someone to blame. His eyes came to rest on Rat. Leopard misjudged his pounce because of the extra weight. Metal shelves came crashing down as the engorged cat chased the rodent around and around the room. The sound of banging metal was deafening, "CLANG, BANG, BANGCLANG, BANG." Soon the faces of angry people appeared in every window and doorway throughout the village.

Rat managed to scurry up a cornstalk and through the thatched roof. Leopard was right behind her. His eyes burned with hatred as he inched closer and closer. Rat ran to the edge of the roof, but there was nowhere else to go. Below, a crowd had gathered around the building. Some villagers had brought long-handled *sungumi* hoes, and torches to see the beast in their midst.

Flames from the torches revealed a desperate Rat about to jump. Then in the shadows something strange took place. Rat leapt high and frantically grabbed at the air. Then the skin that hung at her sides billowed and stretched and her arms became wings. Rat had become the first bat, and she quickly flew into the night on her leathery wings.

Too late, the surprised Leopard turned to face the villagers. One of the torches touched the dry palm fronds of the thatched roof. Flames immediately shot up under Leopard's heavy belly. Sparks and burning embers fell all over his body. Again and again his fine fur was burned.

It took a fierce effort for Leopard to gather himself up. With a terrible scream, "RRAAAOW," he sprang above and over the heads of the villagers, landing heavily as a snarling, smoking mass of pain. His heavy belly swayed back and forth as he ran from the village. Leopard eventually recovered from his ordeal, but his tawny skin still bears the sooty spots of his burns.

Rat—now Bat—still lives at the guava tree, but she is able to rest at the top where the most succulent fruit waits for her. Though Leopard remains as mean as ever, he cannot climb to the top of the tree and is a threat no longer.

—Based on a story told by Sani Isa

Komi nisan jifa kasa zai fadi.
He who laughs last, laughs longest.

Bello, the leather worker, looked up from his work. He had stretched two strips of bright red Sokoto leather, and was expertly punching a row of holes along the edge of one with his long, sharp *kibiya* awl. The other strip lay already finished beside his foot.

Displayed on a mat around Bello's *taitama* anvil were some of the leather products he made. There were leather bags for the Islamic books that the *malams* carried, and skin waterbags and sturdy leather bags for storing or carrying grain.

There were also bags to be hung around horses' necks to feed them guinea corn or millet. Bello also made bridles and saddles and he had constructed the high-backed camel saddles stretched over a frame of wood, though that was really a separate speciality.

At the front of the mat were finely crafted bags for barbers to carry their razors and knives. The barbers needed special bags because they did much more than cut hair. These specially trained barbers were also skilled at cutting facial tribal markings so that people then could always display their heritage.

Musa absent-mindedly examined a new style of feedbag cut from softer leather, which could be bent to funnel in more grain while an animal was eating.

"Are you planning to modernize your transportation?" joked Amina.

"Go on, laugh all you want. Once I was stuck at the motor park in Shinkafi for two days. I would rather ride a nice, dependable donkey than wait for a lorry or a bus!" said Musa.

Bello examined the leather strips with a keen eye. The years of painstaking detail he had put into his craft were told by the deep lines etched on his face. He scooped some *tuwo* from the hollow of his *deleb* palm nut shell and carefully dabbed it onto the two pieces of hide. The *tuwo,* besides being good to eat, would stick the leather together long enough for him to start the stitching.

"Soon this will be a fine sheath for a sword. A man still needs to look after himself when he takes his goats or cattle from place to place. You never know, maybe it will protect a herder or a trader like you, Musa. In fact, it reminds me of a story of a trader like you. Perhaps one of your ancestors," the leather worker smiled as he started the story.

Millipede and Tortoise Make a Trade

In the olden days people did not have all the fine things they have today. Trade goods from far away places were difficult to get. In order to obtain things a person had to travel by narrow, lonely roads to the city. Trading was not protected by laws, the way it is now. Traders had to be very brave and resourceful because many armed robbers lay in waiting in the bushes along the trail. The bandits would as soon kill a merchant as not, and many people who set out for other towns did not return.

In a small, remote village lived an ordinary millipede who had a very ambitious wife. More than anything else she wanted to be rich. The wife wanted her husband to take their savings to the village beyond the hills and buy spices, which could be traded so profitably at their market.

Unfortunately, millipedes cannot see. They squirm about in all directions and arrive anywhere by chance. To safely find the village beyond the hills and return seemed all but impossible and Millipede was afraid.

Millipede always made excuses to his wife for not making the journey. He always promised that he would go the next day. And each day he would be too afraid to set out. Finally his wife called him a coward.

Millipede turned to his wife saying, "Do not talk to me that way. Do you not know that before you met me, I killed a lion with my bare hands? I am the greatest warrior who ever lived. I have beaten twenty men at a time!"

Millipede rushed off, furious and humiliated. Of course, in his sightless condition it was not long before he collided with someone. It was Tortoise, the wealthy village business-man and moneylender.

"My friend," said Tortoise, "You are not equipped to travel so quickly."

Millipede agreed. "Yes, it is a miserable state to be in, and especially now that I need to make an important journey. My good friend Tortoise, if you will lend me your eyes, I will return them next week and pay you well for them."

Tortoise, always ready to do business, took the eyes from his head and handed them over. Millipede thanked Tortoise and hurried back to his wife. He told her what had hap-pened and gave her one eye. He put one eye in his head and she put the other one in hers. Immediately they could both see! Mrs. Millipede squealed with joy and said, "Now you have no excuse. You must start the journey at once."

Millipede agreed to set out that very day, but only if his wife would accompany him so that she could witness how brave he was. He secretly thought that if there was trouble along the road, her quick tongue would surely get her killed. Then if he was still alive, he would return and marry a less annoying millipede, or even a centipede.

So Millipede and his wife wrapped up their money and some local crafts. Millipede equipped himself with a cutlass and a sturdy club and loaded his donkey with sugar cane. Then, delighted with themselves and their prospects, the mil-lipedes wiggled out of the village and along the hillside trail.

Millipede led the donkey by a rope while his wife followed along behind. They had walked only a few hours
when a robber suddenly emerged from the bushes. He stood
so tall and was so huge that he completely blocked the path.
The wife was pleased that now her husband would prove
how brave he was by dealing with the bandit. But instead of
fighting with the robber, Millipede forgot about his weapons
and stood shaking where he was.

Mrs. Millipede was surprised by what she saw, and as
usual began taunting her husband. "Go on," she called. "Are
you not Millipede who killed a lion with his bare hands?
Are you not the greatest warrior who ever lived, the one
who has beaten twenty men at a time?"

The thief, on hearing all this, began to fear for his life.
He dove into the bushes and ran away. The millipedes had
no further trouble because the bandit went before them.
When he met other robbers he warned all of them about the
dangerous many-legged warrior and his wife. As the story
was told and retold, the greatness of Millipede's feats in-
creased until people trembled at the sound of his name.

The trading journey was a great success. Millipede and
his wife were able to return with a heavy donkey-load of
spices, which brought a fine price at the market. However,
Mrs. Millipede now refused to return the borrowed eyes to
Tortoise. "We are rich and I am beautiful. Why should we
not enjoy the sight of all that we have?" So the millipedes
settled down to enjoy their new life of luxury.

Tortoise could do nothing but sit in front of his house
and wait. He held a string to guide him back to his door. In

those days Tortoise often came out of his house and he did not take it everywhere with him. He trusted people and left his house unguarded. Ever since the treachery of the millipedes, Tortoise has been suspicious of everyone and takes his house with him wherever he goes.

As Tortoise rested there lamenting his eyeless condition, he heard none other than Millipede and his wife scurrying by on their way to the marketplace. Tortoise quickly scooted back into his house. "My, my," he called out as they began to pass. "You certainly sound lovely today, Mrs. Millipede!"

Mrs. Millipede came to a stop at once. "Thank you, sir. And who might you be?" she blushed happily.

"I am only *Kunkuru,* a humble weaver's stone of course," replied Tortoise. And indeed he looked exactly like a smooth stone.

Mrs. Millipede was disappointed. "Oh, what can a weaver's stone know of beauty?" she said.

"Alas, it is true that I cannot gaze upon your beauty. It saddens me terribly. Would you and your generous husband lend me your eyes that I may appreciate your loveliness?" he asked sweetly.

No sooner were the two eyes handed over than Tortoise popped them back into his head. He was so delighted to see again that he spared the millipedes the punishment they deserved and accepted his money back with interest.

To this day the millipedes squirm about in the strangest way. Most creatures have learned to be wary of them and leave them alone. And since that time, no bandit has dared to block the road to the village. All the villagers are free to trade wherever they wish. The village is now a great trading city and everyone there lives in comfort and peace.

—Based on a story told by Mohammed Jubril

Mugu shi ya san makwantar mugu.
Set a thief to catch a thief.

All heads turned to look as a car horn blasted behind them. The crowd of shoppers parted to each side as a gray Mercedes crept forward. It pushed its way to the edge of the marketplace where fresh meat was sold. There, vendors sat at tables of bamboo where cuts of beef and goat meat were displayed. In front of some tables were the heads of the animals to identify which was for sale. The vendors were doing a good business, even in the afternoon heat, which seemed unable to keep either hungry customers or dark clouds of flies away.

A distinguished-looking man got out of the car and strode across the marketplace. From the new *zannabukar* fez on his head, to his flowing *riga* with its gold threads, down to his patent leather shoes he was clearly an *Alhaji,* probably a successful businessman. The man walked directly to a tall, thin figure, who stood quietly by the nearest butcher's stall. Next to the tall man, a younger man in blue jeans and a jaunty felt hat used an axe to hack apart a rack of ribs. The tall man seemed not to notice as bits of fat and bone flew up with each blow, scattering the flies.

The tall man was a *Fulani* herdsman. He wore blue robes with black embroidery and carried the herdsman's walking staff. A turban of white cloth wrapped carefully around his head, under his chin, and around his neck protected him from the sun. He wore plain leather sandals that long journeys had molded to his feet. The two men greeted each other formally and spoke at length. Then the businessman took out a huge roll of *naira* from his pocket, counted out several bills and handed them to the herdsman.

The men parted company and the Fulani herdsman came over to the group of storytellers. Ibrahim greeted the newcomer warmly. *"Barka da rana* my friend, Ali from the open roads. How goes your journey?

"Sannu, Allah watches over me, Ibrahim. And you? How is your work?" Ali asked.

"I have not wasted all week listening to these thieves steal my time. I have made the stove we spoke of." With that, Ibrahim reached into his bag and drew out a curious dish-shaped object, made from an oil drum, with a base constructed of elaborately curved metal strips. Ibrahim held it up by a chain fastened on two sides.

The herdsman smiled as Ibrahim handed the stove to him. He turned it this way and that as he studied the fine craftsmanship. The structure was solid, and shaped to hold enough coal to cook a large meal, but still it fit easily in his hands.

"You have done well, Ibrahim—as usual. This stove is as light as it is strong. It will be as nothing until I need it," Ali smiled.

As Ali counted the money to pay Ibrahim, he stepped forward and his robe parted to reveal a long thin knife at his side. It was undoubtedly Ibrahim's work. There was no need for a signature. The curved metal of the hilt matched the curved metal strips on the stove exactly. Like the stove, it could be carried effortlessly by a man walking with his herd from morning until night, day after day.

"Those are fine long-horned cattle you brought to market this week, Ali. Is the Alhaji buying from you now?" asked Umaru.

"Yes, the trip was long and hot this time. My old bull sired most of the calves in my herd, but this trip was its last.

It is too far for the bull to walk to Sokoto where Alhaji Nad-abo will buy my cattle," explained Ali.

"Isn't Alhaji Nadabo the one they call the 'King of Kerosene'? They say he owns all the kerosene sold in Sokoto State," responded Umaru.

"It's true. Every vendor in every market is selling the Alhaji's kerosene," added Bello.

"Do you know what I heard? I heard that the Alhaji would not be so rich if he did not mix his kerosene with petrol!" whispered Musa.

"How can you say that, Musa? You have never seen the Alhaji mixing his kerosene. You can't tell what's real from the stories you spin," scolded Ali.

"Oh, really? I do not need to see the act. I have seen the result. We have all seen poor Shehu Sanda who was burned almost to death by exploding kerosene. And don't you test your kerosene before you light it?" questioned Musa.

"He has you there, Ali. I've seen you pour a bit of kerosene on the floor and toss a match to it. And more than once I've had mine blow up in my face," said Amina.

"Well, of course you can't be too safe. Why do you think I want Ibrahim's coal stove here?" laughed Ali. "I'd rather cook my food than blow it up."

"Ah, you are wise beyond your years, Ali. It is no wonder that you, too, are becoming a wealthy man. You have so many cattle and goats, and a big family. You have wives to tend the cattle and many children to tend the goats. You are truly blessed, Fulani," observed Ibrahim.

"It is so, thanks be to God," smiled Ali. "Life is good. And better still to have good friends like you. My family will eat hot rice cooked on this stove tonight."

Amina impatiently waved her arm over her pyramids of vegetables. Her jewelry jangled gaily back and forth. "Look at what you have done now, Ali!" joked Amina. "You have brought flies from the meat stalls over to my food. Now I will have to *dash* you the rice I know you would have bought from me."

"How is it you know my thoughts, Amina? It is true I need the rice, but I have money today and you shall have some," Ali laughed.

"Be careful, herdsman, or you will have no money to replace that old bull of yours. If insects were paying customers, Amina would have become richer than the Alhaji long ago," commented Bello.

"Oh, what difference does it make? You need more than a good bull to build a herd. Cows are much more important! Ali, I'm surprised that an experienced herder and husband like you does not know all about that. Why, this little insect knows more than all you men put together," scoffed Amina waving away another fly. "Now listen to my story of what once took place on this very same ancient cattle route from Niamey to Sokoto and I'll show you what I mean."

Louse Joins the Herd

Once there was a poor servant who worked for a rich, powerful herdsman. At the close of a long and tiring season, as the herd approached the end of the trail, the well-dressed, rich man turned to his servant in rags and said, "You have worked well this year and I have not paid you even enough to buy clothes. I will give you something to bring you great status. I will give you a cow."

The rich man examined all his animals as they walked by. It was a fine herd. One by one, the healthy cattle passed. Finally, at the end of the line, an old cow struggled to keep up with the others. It staggered as it walked and its sides heaved—"HAWOOF, HAWOOF"—as it breathed. It is understandable that with such a strange sight in front of them, neither the herdsman, nor the servant noticed a small plume of dust, which rose above a tiny, tiny creature, which followed the old cow.

The herdsman halted the cow with his staff. He traced his fingers across the animal's jutting ribs and hipbones. He took his time as he carefully studied the tired beast. The herdsman was making a great ceremony of the present he was bestowing.

After a while, the tiny creature that had been following the herd gradually caught up and "KATUMP, KATUMP. KATUMP, KATUMP," it crawled up the cow's leg. It was little Louse who had, for the first time, joined the herd. Truly, it did not look as though the cow had long to live.

"Yes, my friend, you deserve your own cow and so you shall have this one," the sly herdsman proclaimed. His poor servant tried to object, but he was ignored. There was nothing for him to do but put a rope on the beast and lead it away.

No sooner had they stepped aside than the cow collapsed "SHEBOOB" on the ground. The servant knelt beside the poor beast and listened for a heartbeat. Frightened, Louse quickly jumped onto the man's shoulder. The mean herdsman threw back his head and laughed, saying that a bargain was a bargain, and payment was finished. But then a surprising thing happened. The old cow suddenly gave birth to a calf. And then, another one!

The servant was shocked, but rejoiced, saying, *"Sosai!* You are right. A bargain is a bargain. Now I am a herdsman like you." Louse began to jump about on the servant's shoulder and sing, " It's true, it's true, it's true. I agree with you!" This was more than the mean herdsman could bear.

"The calves belong to me, you fool. It was my bull, that sired them. They belong to me." He raised his staff to strike the servant. Several people stopped walking to see what would become of the cattle. The servant thought quickly.

"Please don't hurt me. I have to go to my father today to bring him medicine. He gave birth to a baby last night and is not well," the man pleaded.

The herdsman turned to the crowd. "Do you see what a madman he is? Do you believe this fool? How can a man give birth to a child?" The herdsman grabbed the poor man by the arm and demanded, "What do you mean by this foolishness?"

Little Louse jumped from the servant onto the herdsman. The herdsman was distracted by Louse, and started scratching and waving his arms in the air. The crowd was really beginning to enjoy this performance. The herdsman pulled at his fine clothes to scratch underneath them. He hopped back and forth, making faces and muttering to himself. Seeing that everyone had ceased to take the herdsman seriously, the servant pleaded for them to judge his case. He begged, "If a man cannot give birth to a child, how can this herdsman's bull have produced these calves?" Louse became so excited that she jumped from person to person crying, "It's true, it's true, it's true! I agree with you!"

All the villagers called on the herdsman to stop abusing the poor servant, and let him keep the cow and its calves. The herdsman protested that he had given this man his employment and did not deserve to be abandoned after such generosity. Louse jumped back to the herdsman's head and called out, "Let your ungrateful servant go. I will watch over your cattle and never leave you. It's true, it's true, it's true! I agree with you!"

The frustrated herdsman pulled at his hair, cursed at Louse, and walked away. He has been walking and cursing at Louse ever since.

—*Based on a story told by Suleman Zara*

Kowa ya kona runbunsa, ya san inda toka ke kudi ne.
Apparent stupidity can be concealed wisdom.

B̲ello suddenly called out loudly to everyone, "It's my brother's son. Look, he has come from school. You know my brother, Isa. He has sent his son to school, and now the boy is already in secondary school. Doesn't he look good in his school uniform?"

"You can stop waving now, Bello. Your nephew is coming over. I hope he has permission to be off school grounds because they must have heard you calling even back at G.S.S. Gwadabawa," laughed Musa.

"I think Isa must have heard him back in Berni Nkonni. That is, unless the town has been buried by the desert by now. Has the Sahara caught up to the town yet, Bello?" asked Umaru.

"Oh, each year it grows worse, to be sure. But here is young Lawal. Maybe he can sweep the desert back when he returns home! How are you doing, Lawal?" grinned Bello as his nephew came to greet him.

"I am well, Uncle. It is good to see you," said the boy.

"You do look bigger than the last time I saw you. Are they feeding you properly at the school?" asked Ibrahim.

"Ah, it is terrible! Only *gari* and cow stomach," complained Lawal.

"Well, it cannot be too bad if you are growing so tall. We hoped to see you singing the *matukule* at our front door this year. Were you too busy to visit your uncle or could you not find the head of a donkey for your performance?" asked Bello.

"It has been so difficult, Uncle. That is why I have not been able to visit you for so long. We had our state exams this year during *Ramadan*. With fasting from sunrise to sunset each day everyone was too weak even to study," Lawal added.

"Tsk, what a shame. The school should have had exams before Ramadan. That's not fair," said Umaru.

"It was the Ministry that scheduled the exams," said Lawal.

"That makes it worse! How did you do, Lawal?" asked Bello.

"I think I passed them all," smiled Lawal.

"Ah, of course. That is my brother's boy. Did you hear that everyone? Nothing can stop this clever boy! Good work, Lawal!" beamed Bello.

"So what brings you to the market today?" asked Musa.

Lawal's smile faded from his face. "I have to buy *Omo* to wash the library prefect's laundry. He gave me fifty *kobo* and he knows it costs sixty *kobo*. Working for the older Form V boys takes all my time. And now if they misbehave and receive punishment from the duty masters, they want us small boys to serve it!"

"Oh no, that is awful! Then you must work even harder to become a prefect yourself someday. Take this ten kobo until you are a big man," laughed Ibrahim.

"That won't be for two years yet. I will never make it!" moaned Lawal.

"Here Lawal, take some sweets for energy. And here is some rice and onions to cook at night. You need to take care of yourself," said Musa.

"What are you doing, Musa! Those are my onions and rice to give! Of course you should take them, Lawal. And here are some tomatoes, too. Just don't listen to people who give away things that are not theirs!" joked Amina.

"You need to be patient, Lawal, and your day will come. All the work you have done will bring better things to you. Just be patient," advised Bello. "I have a story that you might find interesting. It is just a made-up story . . . a legend from long ago. . . ."

Why Gorilla Lives
in the Jungle

Once, when the world's first generation was still alive, there lived young Gorilla who was very unhappy. Gorilla was strong and fierce. He had great, muscular arms and long pointed teeth. He could tear down trees with his bare hands and throw great boulders with ease. Yet he was sad and lonely.

One day Gorilla could stand it no longer. He went to a quiet place on top of a mountain to pray to God. Gorilla pleaded with God, "Life is so unfair. I have to stay in the jungle all the time. My house is nothing but a few bent branches and grass. The rain falls on me and I am cold at night. I can barely find enough food to eat. Gorillas suffer and yet humans receive all the sweetness of the world. Why must I be an animal when I could be a human being?"

God decided He would make Gorilla a human being if Gorilla could wait patiently for seven days for Him to do it. If Gorilla could live in the jungle, unseen by Man for just seven days, then he could live forever after in the comfort of human society.

Gorilla eagerly promised to fulfill his part of the bargain. Then he bounded off, crashing through the jungle to begin his first day of waiting. Gorilla spent the day picking and eating leaves and fruit. At night he curled up in his nest and dreamed of his future life in town with all the fine people of the village.

On the second, third, fourth, and fifth days Gorilla foraged for food with his family, groomed himself, and stared off into the distance, imagining what his new house would be like; his friends and neighbors. Then on the sixth day Gorilla was so overjoyed, so proud of his patience, that he could contain his excitement no longer. He began dancing and slapping his hands on the ground. The ground shook and trees trembled as he rushed forward, snorting and bellowing like a water buffalo. He beat his great chest and flung out his massive arms to challenge the world.

Gorilla danced his way right into the village of Man. "I will be one of you tomorrow! Make room for me. I am here to stay!" he shouted. Gorilla twirled about the marketplace, sending tables and food flying in all directions. The startled townspeople fell over each other trying to get out of his way. They ran and hid, fearing for their lives.

Gorilla called for the people to come out. The more he looked for them, the more afraid and desperate they became. After a while, an angry group of villagers attacked Gorilla all at once. They threw rocks at him and beat him with long poles. After a terrible fight, the confused and beaten Gorilla retreated back to the jungle.

On the seventh day, God returned to Gorilla and told him, "It saddens me to say that you have not kept your part of the bargain. You are too impatient and cannot control yourself. It is better that you live in the jungle, where you cannot hurt anyone and where you will be safe."

Since that day, Gorilla has always stayed in the jungle. He prefers life in the mountains where he can be left alone. Though he looks like Man, he is wild and belongs in the jungle.

—Based on a story told by Bankole Adedaya

Kashin turmi ba na wadan kare ba ne.
Do not attempt what is beyond your powers to perform.

Over at the meat vendors' stalls, a large group of people was gathering. A drummer beat his drum to announce the arrival of visitors. The village was being challenged to a *Kwambala!*

A team of wrestlers had arrived from Zaria. The young men all had the long uncut hair of a wrestler. Some had rings in one ear; others wore a cap with two flaps to cover the ears. They moved with the natural grace of athletes, and their lean, muscular bodies stood out in the crowd. They looked impressive in their sleeveless *falmaras* shirts wrapped in black cloth. Around their waists were leather *warki* aprons decorated with round belts of leather and hanging amulets for protection.

The wrestling match would take place later at the village arena. This afternoon the men were asking for donations of food around the market, and letting everyone know that superior athletes were in town. The younger boys stood at the back and carried the two-handled grass bags of the older ones. Lawal quickly said goodbye to his uncle and ran over to talk to one of the younger boys. One after another, vendors welcomed the wrestlers and gave them food, knowing that their own team would receive the same treatment in other towns.

Ibrahim ignored the wrestlers and continued with his work. Everyone remembered what a famous wrestler Ibrahim had been in his youth. Now his shaved head signified that he was a veteran wrestler, one of the *Gumburai* who had retired with distinction.

Ibrahim was still a powerful wrestler. Just a few years before, not long after he retired, a visiting team had badly beaten the village wrestlers. It was a humiliating defeat. Then the drummer called Ibrahim's drum beat. Ibrahim answered the challenge. He powdered his face with indigo and entered the arena. Ibrahim wrestled and beat the leader of the visiting team by throwing him back so that his arm touched the ground. Ibrahim was the hero of the village that day and was showered with presents.

These days, Ibrahim seemed content to be a blacksmith. But as the others glanced at his face, they could see the longing in his eyes for the glory days. Now his son had begun wrestling, and no father could be more proud.

"When my son wrestles tomorrow he will send these challengers home quickly," said Ibrahim.

"You are *Gumburai*. Will you enter the arena?" asked Amina.

"Someone needs to show these young people how to wrestle with passion. They are too cautious!" complained Umaru.

"Oh really! And aren't you two the ones who are always saying that young people need to learn patience?" laughed Amina.

"Not in wrestling. That is another matter. There is a time for everything," Umaru scowled.

"The *Gumburai* have had their time. The boys will learn for themselves, and if we are fortunate they will teach us things some day. They will be here for us when our strength is gone and theirs is great," Ibrahim smiled.

"This reminds me of a story that I heard when I was only a boy," he began.

Ostrich in the Desert

In the great desert to the north there is a small town where no one lives now. Once there were many people there. We know this because they built mud houses and a high wall around the town. This is the story of what happened to them.

Even in the old days, the desert was always a place where life was hard. Food was scarce, the winds could flay the skin from your body and the heat of the midday sun could kill you where you stood. The desert stretched farther than an animal could travel, and to leave the water behind was to die.

Where there was water, life surrounded it. Near the middle of the desert, a crack in the earth bubbled with cool spring water. This pool of water, flowing year round, created an oasis with grass and fig trees and a tall palm nearby.

The oasis was the home of Ostrich and her brood of three chicks. They were all black and gray exactly like their mother, except that one was much smaller than the others. In those days ostriches did not have long necks or legs. There was really only one kind of bird, and it had a short neck, short legs, and wings so small that it could not fly. Birds were the favorite prey of most desert animals because they were not strong enough or fast enough to escape.

Whenever Mother Ostrich found food she would call her chicks over to eat. But her voice could not be heard above the desert winds, which howled day and night. To call them she would stretch out her small wing and beckon to the first chick, which was the eldest. Then she would stretch out her other wing and beckon to the second chick, which was the next eldest. But when it was the third chick's turn to be summoned, Mother Ostrich had no more wings. She did not beckon for the third chick. The small one usually did not feed with the others and became weaker with each passing day.

One day, a hungry lion walked across the sands to the oasis. He lay down and watched the ostriches intently from far away. He saw how Mother Ostrich stretched her wings to call her chicks.

Lion visited the spring and took a long drink. The cool water soothed his parched throat and made his voice sound sweet and smooth. When Mother Ostrich went looking for food, the young ones hid in the grass. Lion used his sweetest voice to call out to them, "WOOOOW, WOOOOW. It is supper time." But they stayed hidden where they were with their short necks and legs tucked under their wings. Then Lion remembered the beckoning of Mother Ostrich. He thought about how she moved her wings and how the chicks came to her.

Now Lion circled so that he stood with his back to the wind. He turned his head to the side as he called, and the wind blew his shaggy mane to the side just like the ostrich's wing. The first chick jumped up and ran to Lion. He turned his head so that the wind blew his mane the other way. The second chick jumped up and ran to him. Lion pounced on them and ate them up in two bites.

A third time Lion shook his head and waved his mane in the wind. The third chick was confused because she had never been called before. She slowly came forward but stopped before she was too close. Lion leapt forward and snapped his jaws shut. But he only held Young Ostrich's head in his jaws. She pulled and pulled and finally her tiny head slipped out, "SHOOOP," from between his teeth. She tumbled backwards and scampered away as quickly as her short legs would allow.

Lion fell back and watched with disgust as she put some distance between them. The puny bird was not worth chasing. Young Ostrich now had a long neck. She could see her mother far away and ran to her.

For protection against predators like Lion, Ostrich and her daughter joined a group of animals that was beginning to build a town around the oasis. These animals wanted to be strong and powerful. They collected many weapons like machetes, swords, and spears. They worked hard to dig mud and mix it with chopped *guinea corn* stalks. They rolled the mud into large balls and stacked the balls one on top of the other. They piled the balls higher and higher to make a wall, which eventually circled all the way around the oasis.

The animals wanted to be still stronger and more powerful. They dressed as warriors and trained for battle. Finally they decided that only the young warriors should remain in the town. All their elders were rounded up and pushed outside the wall. The warriors told each other that the old ones would be fine outside the walls and they forgot about them.

Young Ostrich did not believe that the old ones would be safe. With her long neck she could see out over the wall where they were dying of thirst. Young Ostrich did not push her mother out. She hid her mother in a basket and used a rope to pull it high into the palm tree. At night she would lower the basket and share her food with her mother.

One night the others heard the basket coming down. They attacked Young Ostrich with their weapons. She ran round and round the palm. With each turn her legs grew longer and stronger. The animals threw their machetes, swords, and spears at the basket. The weapons fell back to earth, and hit the others standing below. This enraged everyone. Shouting turned to fighting. All the warriors were ready for battle. The animals did not stop until they had killed one another.

Mother Ostrich was knocked out of the basket. As she fell to earth she flapped her wings and began to fly. She was the first bird to fly and now many birds can fly. Young

Ostrich followed her mother out of the compound. With her powerful legs she kicked down the gate, "KEEER-AAAK," and ran away. She is still the fastest runner in the desert.

The walled town in the desert has been deserted ever since. Sand has blown in and covered much of the town. The wall is still there. But there is no one to keep out, and no one wants to live there.

—Based on a story by Adamu Tukur

Ba a shan zuma sai an sha harbi.
Success comes after tears.

"If your son is going to wrestle tomorrow, I hope he has been to see Tsalla," said Amina.

Tsalla sat across from Ibrahim. The various herbs she sold for traditional medicine were spread out on a blanket in front of her. Tsalla was a big woman with plaited hair and henna tattoos on her hands and feet. Though she was not a doctor, she had a great knowledge of local plants and how to use them.

Tsalla had helped many people through their illnesses. She was well known and very popular both in town and throughout the more remote bush regions.

Umaru the weaver shook his head sadly and spat at a fly about to land on his cloth. "Oh, of course, ask the Bush Woman to brew up an instant solution to make the wrestlers win. If it burns your skin or tastes bad she knows all about it. The trouble is that wrestling takes a long time to master, even with the right teachers. Young people are in too much of a hurry these days," he said.

Then, too late he remembered the amulet that hung around his neck to keep him safe. He had bought it from

Tsalla and never took it off. Everyone chuckled as he tried to cover it with his shirt. He rubbed the shirt material between his finger and thumb.

"It is a pity that no one respects this handwoven Hausa cloth anymore. Why is it that only old men like myself take the trouble to weave beautiful black *saki* cloth and the sparkling *tsamiya* gowns? Do you think young people bother to collect silk from the silkworm? Are they going to climb up into the *tamarind* tree to get it? No, everyone goes to the modern shops. They think that is where silk comes from! These days everything is made by new machines."

Umaru grinned at Tsalla and then at the rest of the group. "I talk too much. But you all know how much I respect this Bush Woman and her talents. Tsalla and I both fear how much traditional knowledge will be lost if we forget the wisdom of the past. Soon the old ways will be gone. Listen to the wisdom that comes from the old ways while you can."

How Man Found a Friend

O nce upon a time a hunter was searching through the bush for game. He suddenly came upon a large snake trapped under a boulder. The snake twisted and rolled and bit its own tail, but it could not get free.

The snake implored, "My dear kind friend, will you please help me?"

The hunter hesitated. "If I help you, how do I know you won't bite me? A snake is a snake, and a man is a man. It is your nature to kill me."

"Oh, that will never happen! You are the greatest of creatures. I crawl on my belly before you. You have nothing to fear from me," assured the snake.

The hunter bent down and slowly raised the heavy stone off the snake. Then the snake raised up his narrow head and spat, "So I am free at last! You know there is no agreement between myself and your people. You are not my brother. I will kill you now."

"Wait! I know it is your nature to kill me and that I was foolish to help you, but in this special case can you not spare me since I saved your life?" pleaded the hunter.

"No," replied the snake. "A snake is a snake, and a man is a man. Now I must bite you and you must die."

The hunter made a final, desperate suggestion. "Do what you must. But let your brothers speak to decide what is natural and right. If you agree, we will go before three judges and allow them to decide if I should die."

"Very well," agreed the snake. "We will ask the first three creatures we meet along the road and they shall decide your fate."

As they set out along the road, a huge bull elephant suddenly emerged from the trees. Seeing the man, he raised his trunk and trumpeted a warning, "AHROOOAH, AHROOOAH!" The snake hailed him as his brother and said, "Elephant, if you have knowledge of Man, speak now and be heard."

The elephant came forward and stared down at the hunter. "You should kill this man," said Elephant. "My people remember how long ago Man lived near elephants in peace. We respected each other and each thrived on the gifts of the world. Then Man decided he wanted to make pretty things from our tusks. He chased us from our lands and hunted us until now the great elephant herds are gone and we hide in the forest in fear. So my advice to you is to kill this man quickly before he kills you."

The snake thanked Brother Elephant for his advice. "Your words are wise and you have been heard." Then turning to the hunter he said, "You see I am right. This judge is on my side. Let us continue."

They had not gone far, when they heard a monkey chattering high in a baobab tree, "CHEECHEECHEEK!" Snake hailed him as his brother and called for him to judge their case, saying, "If you have knowledge of Man speak now and be heard."

When the monkey heard the story he shrieked, "Why can't you kill this man? You know, once Man was our brother. Then he took up his front legs and started walking around on his other two legs. He burned off the hair which covered his body. Where is his tail? You see he cut off his tail because he did not want to look like us. At first he made us work for him. But later, even that disgusted him and he started killing us. I advise you to kill this man."

The snake thanked Brother Monkey, "Your words are wise and you have been heard." Then Snake turned to the hunter and said, "The second judge is on my side. There remains only the opinion of the third judge. Let us continue." The hunter grew even more worried.

They continued until they came across a dog lying by the side of the road. They greeted him and related their story. Snake invited him, "If you have knowledge of Man, speak and you shall be heard."

Brother Dog howled, "AAHOOOOO!" when he told of how he was alone and rejected by mankind. Yet he protested, "I cannot judge this case without seeing the spot where it began." So the three of them went back to the stone together.

Dog turned to Snake. "In what condition did he find you?"

"He saw this heavy stone lying on top of me," the snake informed him.

"Is that true?" the dog asked the hunter.

"Exactly true," agreed the hunter. "The snake could not move under the weight of the stone, so I removed it."

"In that case, Snake, lie down as you were before." The snake did as he was told. "Now Man, you roll the stone back to the original position."

When it was done Dog inquired, "Is this how the man found you?" The snake, unable to move, agreed that it was so.

"Good. Now wait for another man to come along and help you." Then the dog turned to the man saying, "A dog is only a dog, and a man is only a man. Let us be friends and hunt together."

When Snake realized what had happened, he twisted and stretched and struck furiously at the air. He cursed himself for not having killed the man immediately and bit at his own tail, but it was too late. He could not get free. Perhaps he is there still. If you do see Snake, be careful, for he has never forgiven Man and is quick to bite.

That is the story of why hunters and dogs remain together. And that is the reason for their friendship. That is why you cannot beat a dog near his master. And if you challenge his master near him, the dog will bite you. It is his nature.

—*Based on a story told by Aminu Manuga*

Idan wata ta koni mutum, in ya ga toka sai ya gudu.
Once bitten, twice shy.

The marketplace itself seemed to shift and stretch as vendors here and there packed up their goods and quietly went on their way. Long evening shadows quickly flowed over the flat landscape, blending together and settling around the people who remained, as the red glow of sunset gave way to growing darkness.

One by one, kerosene bush lamps sputtered to life. The smoke from a burning mosquito repellent coil rose slowly with a rhythmic, snake-like motion that reminded everyone of the snake and the hunter. The cooler night air seemed especially still. It was a relief after the sweltering heat of the day. In the stillness of the evening the marketplace seemed hushed and peaceful.

Nearby, a circle of *sooya* sticks planted around an open fire sizzled as the tantalizing aroma of spiced meat, onions, and peppers filled the air. Musa bought several sticks of *sooya* and came back with the meat wrapped in brown paper. He passed the food around to everyone. Musa was chewing a *kolanut* flavored with orange syrup and he was in a

good mood. The old potter laughed, showing a mouthful of
orange teeth.

"Ah, there is nothing like fresh-cooked *sooya*—it is a
work of art. In fact it reminds me of a story I heard once at
the Crop Festival in Kaduna," he said.

The Carver and the Panther

In the middle of a dark jungle lived a carver of great reputation. People came from cities far away to buy his wonderful ebony carvings. However, the man remained poor since he devoted so much time and care to each statue.

One day the carver went to the bush to find ebony wood for his next carving. This was to be his greatest statue ever. When he came upon a tall ebony tree with magnificent branches, his experienced eye saw that this was the perfect wood. The carver raised his axe. Every stroke was placed with precision. No surgeon could cut with more expert care. After several swift blows, the ebony tree came crashing down.

When the tree lay on the ground the carver was surprised to see the body of a freshly killed antelope wedged between the branches.

"Well, fortune is smiling on me today. I will have the best wood for my carving and good food for myself, and my neighbors," he said as he cut off a large section of a branch. Then he heaved the antelope carcass onto his shoulder and dragged the tree limb back to the village.

Later that day, a panther returned to the spot where the tree lay. This was the tree that had been her home and the antelope was to have been her meal. She had paid dearly for the meat. When she had struggled with the antelope, its horn pierced her side. She had gone to a cool stream nearby to soothe the wound. Now the torn flesh hung open at her side and flies buzzed around it.

The panther was clearly not able to hunt again. With no food or a place to lay up she could easily die here herself. But this was no ordinary panther. In her eye was the sparkle of a *jinn* and she could take the form of a human. The panther removed her skin and became a beautiful woman. She clutched her wounded side as her resistance to pain was now much less. But her animal instinct was still strong and she had no trouble following the trail the carver had left.

As the woman neared the village the tracks were lost among the footsteps of many villagers. She spied an old *calabash* lying beside the path. The round gourd was the size of a basket, but the hole at the top was not much bigger than a coin. She deftly slipped her panther skin into the gourd and strode into the marketplace.

The men of the village immediately crowded around, offering to marry this enchanting creature, sleek and graceful as a cat. The woman managed a smile, but refused to listen to their pleas. She announced that there was no bride price for her. Her parents wanted neither money nor gifts. If any man desired to marry her, he must first pass a simple test. The man she would marry would be the one who could throw a stone into her calabash from six paces away.

Many men tried to throw a stone into the small opening of the calabash. All failed in their attempts. The cunning woman was sure that the man who had cut down her tree with such artful strokes would be able to throw a stone accurately. She called out for anyone who had still not tried his skill.

No one else came forward, so at last the woman reluctantly picked up the calabash and began to leave the village. As she neared the gates she spied the carver, sitting at his work using his *makodi* knife to smooth the wood. She invited him to test his prowess.

He refused, saying, "I am just a poor carver. I have no money and few possessions. One of your beauty is not for me."

The woman insisted, "My parents ask for no bride price, no gifts. But only the man who can throw a stone into this calabash will be my husband."

The carver could not believe that this was true, but decided to go along with it. He chose a stone that felt good in his hand and expertly sent it flying directly into the hole in the calabash. The woman smiled and stepped forward. The carver was incredulous at obtaining such a beautiful bride so easily. As the strange woman took his hand in hers she leaned close to him. Something about the scent of this man was familiar. Mixed with it was the smell of her lost meal. She thought, soon enough this man could become my meal. But first she whispered, "THIS IS MY WISH: TO KISS YOUR LIPS."

The couple was married immediately and the woman moved into the carver's tiny hut. There was enough room for both of them, because the woman brought nothing with her but her calabash and the room contained almost no belongings. There were carving tools and some finished pieces in one corner, some cooking pots, a bed, and a mat in front of the bed for the carver's old dog to sleep on.

Life could have been good for the woman since she was safe and she had enough to eat, but the tame life of the village was not for her. On their wedding night, as the carver lay sleeping the woman arose, put on her skin, and changed into a panther. Her teeth grew long and pointed. Her claws became as sharp as razors. But before she could reach the carver to kill him, the old dog stood up and began barking.

The panther feared that the villagers would run to help the carver if he called out, so she changed back to a woman just as the carver awoke. She told him that there was nothing wrong and that the dog was barking at shadows. The carver scolded the dog and went back to sleep. Again and again the woman tried to change into a panther, and each time the faithful dog warned its master.

In the morning the woman was angry. "Please put the dog outside tonight. I need to get some sleep," she said.

"But the dog is just getting used to you. It has always slept by my bed. Tonight will be better," the carver protested.

"No," snarled the woman. "I have a strong fear of dogs. They don't like me. I cannot sleep next to the dog."

The carver reluctantly gave in and that night he shut the dog outside. But the dog kept sniffing at the door. Whenever the woman changed into a panther, the dog howled and scratched until the carver awoke.

The next morning the woman was more upset than before. Although her wound was healing and she had regained her strength, she knew that she would never be able to kill the carver in the house while his dog was near him. Then the carver solved her problem for her by saying, "I must go into the jungle to chop wood for my carvings. Don't worry, I have already found the ideal tree."

The woman winced at the mention of her destroyed home, but her voice kept a steady purr. "This works out wonderfully. I need to collect wood for cooking. I will come with you. Only, please leave your dog locked in the house. It frightens me so. I am sure it does not like me."

The carver thought this was not true, but kept the dog locked in the house when he prepared to leave. The dog whined and scratched, but the carver ignored it.

Together, husband and wife walked deep into the jungle. The man was proud and excited that he would soon be sharing the secrets of his work with the one he loved. The woman's eyes narrowed and sparkled as she planned a deadly surprise of her own. She whispered, "THIS IS MY WISH: TO KISS YOUR LIPS."

They walked for some time before reaching the felled ebony tree. The carver climbed up high onto one of the branches and began hacking off a suitable limb. The woman circled around the tree, looking for firewood. Then the carver heard a low, throaty growl. He looked down and saw that his wife was gone. Around the tree circled a menacing panther. The carver prayed that his wife had somehow escaped the cat.

The terrified man yelled and screamed but no one could hear. Only the old dog was listening for its master's call for help. Only the dog could hear it. Chunks of mud and plaster broke off the hut wall as the dog squeezed around the door and through a space too small for a rat to pass.

All the neighbors came out to see what the commotion was about. They threw rocks at the noisy dog and chased it out of the village. It had disturbed their sleep for the last time! They chased it until it led them to the ebony tree where the carver remained trapped. The panther was clinging halfway up the branch.

The big cat whirled and snarled. As the village men froze for an instant with their weapons raised, the panther leapt past them and disappeared into the jungle.

The old dog sniffed at the spot where the woman had become an animal. Everyone could plainly see that her tracks had changed into those of the panther.

The carver was stunned. He returned to the village in a daze. Eventually he was able to resume his work, but he was never the same. Something inside him had changed forever. From that time on he carved only panthers. His greatest statue became a panther, black and sleek as liquid night. He could not stop loving she who had been his wife, and in his mind the memories gnawed at him like an animal.

—*Based on a story told by Saidu Mohammed*

Ba kullum a ke kwana a gado ba wata
rana ko a kasa sai a kwana.
Life is a mixture of the sweet and the bitter.

"I'm still hungry. Who wants some *chop?*" asked Bello.

"Buy it from Mustapha. He has the best smoked fish in town," said Amina.

"I heard that Mustapha won a new Peugot at the Argungu Fishing Festival," said Musa.

"Mustapha with a new car? We would have heard all about it by now!" scoffed Amina.

"There are some things that even you do not hear, Amina. Mustapha can't swim, but he was floating on his *calabash,* out in the middle of the Argungu River. He had the biggest fish right in his *koma* net when it got away. I heard that it slapped him in the face with its tail as it swam off. It swam right into Abdul Zagga's net and he won the car," Bello explained.

"Well, I saw someone who looked like Mustapha driving a Peugot," insisted Musa.

"Go on then, Musa. Ask him how he likes driving his new Peugot. Do you think he will give you a ride in the car? More likely he will give you a smack on your head with a smoked fish!" laughed Amina.

"Ha, maybe Tsalla has some medicine to protect against smoked fish," suggested Bello.

"Of course I do. I have gathered herbs from all over the lowlands. There are places along the river that can only be reached by small boat where the people still follow pagan ways. I have seen villages where they practice strange and secret rituals and claim wicked powers you do not want to know about. Listen to this story and just imagine yourself in such a place," Tsalla said.

Tortoise Meets the River Goddess

In a rural district far away downriver there lived a tortoise who had a yam farm. He lived a quiet life in town and never bothered anyone. Each year when harvest came he would load his little boat with yams and set out upriver to a remote village. What no one knew was that Tortoise changed when he left town. He became a wild and carefree creature. While at home he was a respectable land tortoise who never went in the water. But when he was on the river he turned into a river turtle who could swim like a fish, and go anywhere.

The remote village where Tortoise traded his yams was so primitive that the people did not grow anything. They fished for their food and worshipped snakes.

As Tortoise paddled up the river, he thought about what a good year it had been. The boat was full of yams and soon he would be celebrating.

Tortoise came to a spot where the river narrowed and the water flowed quickly. As the water rushed through the narrows, the waves churned and rocked the little boat. Suddenly one of the yams rolled over the side and fell "KU-POOSH" into the water.

Tortoise could not bear to part with even one of his yams. He beached the boat and stood looking at the spot where the yam had disappeared. After some time he resolved to risk another yam to get back his first. He would throw it into the river and follow the current wherever it went.

Tortoise tossed in the second yam and plunged in after it. Now a river turtle, Tortoise could indeed swim like a fish. The yam and Tortoise were both immediately carried down to the river bottom. The current twisted and turned, but Tortoise kept the yam in sight as they continued deeper and deeper. The yam tumbled through the murky depths until finally it came to rest in a deep crevice where the river goddess lived.

This goddess was both beautiful and terrible. She was wonderful to behold but her power to punish was fearful. The river goddess welcomed Tortoise and asked why he had come to her domain. Tortoise told her the whole sad story of his lost yam and how much it meant to him. He begged her to return it.

The river goddess explained that she had found the first yam at her doorstep and that she was cooking it for supper. She thanked Tortoise for the yam and told him to enter her palace of river grasses and accept a gift from her, which would feed him whenever he asked. She instructed, "Take the magic calabash covered in *cowrie* shells, but leave the spoon alone."

"Oh, thank you. I have many magic calabashes in my palace at home," Tortoise boasted. The truth was that Tortoise had no knowledge of real magic and he lived in a modest mud house.

The river goddess pointed to the palace with a finger that ended in a long and twisting nail. Her hair and robes flowed around her with a ghostly aura. She repeated, "Take the magic calabash covered in cowrie shells, but leave the spoon alone."

Tortoise collected the calabash as he was granted and returned to his boat. He resumed his journey upriver and eventually reached the remote fishing village. Statues and pictures of serpents were everywhere. Tortoise was greeted with open arms, and a great celebration began at once. With a flourish, Tortoise ordered the magic calabash to prepare a feast for himself and his friends. This it did, and everyone ate and drank and danced for days. At the end of the feast the chief sent for Tortoise.

The chief was in his hut, which rested at the top of a hill behind two gigantic termite mounds taller than a man. In the center of the room sat the chief on an elaborately ornate stool. Each leg of the stool was the intricately carved like-ness of a curled snake. In his hand the chief held a staff that was shaped like a snake. The staff was rigid and brittle, and its dull scales had no life in them. But as Tortoise ap-proached, the golden eyes of the snake staff seemed to follow his every move.

The chief smiled and asked Tortoise to use the calabash to conjure up a statue of a snake made of solid gold. He wanted the snake to be large enough to coil around his hut and stretch to the sky.

"Oh, I have many magic calabashes and golden statues of my own," boasted Tortoise.

The chief grinned a fiendish grin. "Good, then you can leave this calabash with me after you have performed your magic. There will be another feast tomorrow to mark the occasion."

Something told Tortoise that he should not disappoint the chief. There was evil in the eye of the snake staff and he didn't like it whenever the chief smiled. Yet, when Tortoise commanded the calabash to perform, nothing happened. Then he remembered that the calabash was only intended to feed him. He thought and thought, and then he remem-bered the spoon. The spoon must provide a magic even more powerful, he reasoned, for the goddess was unwilling to part with it.

Making elaborate promises and excuses, Tortoise got back in his boat and returned to where the river goddess lived. This time he deliberately threw a yam into the

water and dove in after it. Tortoise found the goddess and
demanded to trade his yam for another calabash. In spite of
his rudeness, the river goddess was as gracious as before and
instructed, "Enter my palace of river grasses. There you will
find another magic calabash covered in cowrie shells. Take
the calabash, but leave the spoon alone."

Tortoise went into the palace and quickly grabbed the
spoon. He needed more magic than a calabash could give.
Up he swam to the surface and returned to the village in his
boat just as the festival began.

A huge crowd gathered at the chief's hut. They all
brought pots and baskets in case there was any excess food to
take home. At a sign from the chief, *kolanuts* were distrib-
uted to everyone. Then he announced that the main dancer
would be none other than Tortoise himself! Before Tortoise
had time to test the spoon, a team of attendants adorned him
in the skin of a black goat. Amid cheers from the spectators,
Tortoise came forward, his hands held high. One hundred
charms hung from leather bands on his arms.

A drum beat from the *talking drums* called Tortoise to
dance. In his hands he held a ceremonial knife and the
untested spoon. In a great voice he recited a song of praise
for his intelligence and bravery in finding the magic calabash
and the spoon. Tortoise began his victory dance waving the
knife in one hand and the spoon in the other. The knife
blade, which was really beeswax, seemed to melt before
everyone's eyes. The crowd was amazed.

Tortoise paused and asked the chief for permission to turn
the spectators into cattle to provide manure for the chief's

garden. Everyone shrank back to avoid being transformed! They were all relieved when the chief proclaimed that it was time for Tortoise to use his magic to produce the golden statue.

Tortoise was very pleased with himself as he told the mysterious spoon to use its powers.

Suddenly the spoon leapt from his hand and flew about the room, striking everyone, including the chief. The chief's snake-headed staff clattered to the floor and instantly changed into a live and very deadly mamba, which slithered after Tortoise.

Tortoise jumped into a nearby pot. The snake climbed towards the opening, but the spoon knocked the pot over and Tortoise began to roll away. Out of the door he rolled, bumped into the termite mounds, and continued down the slope towards the river. Out of the termite mounds slithered hundreds of snakes. The ground itself seemed to move with writhing bodies. Tortoise kept rolling, pursued by the army of snakes. At the riverbank the pot crashed into Tortoise's boat and broke open. Tortoise scrambled into the boat. He pushed away from the shore just as the fastest serpents tried to crawl up his paddle.

The snakes could not swim and would not enter the water. Tortoise breathed a sigh of relief as he was swept downstream. Then he turned to see that the calabash was floating after him, being paddled furiously by the spoon.

Soon the current became even more powerful. When Tortoise reached the narrows, the boat began to spin. Round and round it turned in the churning water! Suddenly the calabash and spoon were sucked beneath the water and back to the river goddess. At that same moment, Tortoise and his boat were flung away to safety. Tortoise paddled home to his old, respectable life and never brought his yams up the river again.

—*Based on a story by D. Akinfenwa*

Kowa ya daure kura ya san yadda zai yi ya kwance.
Look before you leap.

Bello the leather worker looked surprised and coughed, swallowing the last of his *sooya* with difficulty. "I have to admit, your stories are always strange ones, Tsalla. Tortoise was lucky to escape that time. I almost forgot to chew that *chop*. Now my throat feels sore. We both should have been wearing one of my protective amulets," he said.

Tsalla the herb woman laughed as she adjusted her cloth wrapper around her waist. She kicked off her sandals and sat back to make herself comfortable. Tsalla examined several short twigs before peeling back the end of one and handing it to Bello. "Here, use this chewing stick to clean your teeth before you choke. It is no ordinary stick. It can kill germs as well as any Western medicine," she advised.

Bello deftly twirled the stick between his fingers and thumb to quickly brush his teeth clean. He mimed an ear-to-ear smile to show the results. Tsalla responded by dramatically picking up a bunch of *sabara* shrub, shaking it at Bello, and placing it carefully next to a pile of myrrh. Bello lost his grin, no longer feeling quite so confident.

"You know, these herbs could change your life, leather worker. You should try them. I admit you do make beautiful amulets to hold the protective medicines, but I know which plants to combine to make the medicine powerful. If you want to hear another story of strange creatures and powerful magic, just sit back once more and prepare to be astounded," said Tsalla with a knowing smile.

The Deer Woman

A long time ago, in a house by the edge of the jungle lived a brave hunter named Yakubu. Yakubu had a great reputation throughout the countryside for making long and dangerous hunting trips. On these trips he would sometimes explore places that no one else had ever seen.

One day, Yakubu packed up his bow and quiver and began following a stream, which led far into the thick jungle. Yakubu traveled all day and into the night. By nightfall, the trail he followed was no more than scraps of fruit dropped by birds and monkeys from the branches high above. On the ground the dense tangle of vegetation seemed untouched by man or beast. Yakubu remembered that this jungle had always been known as a place where no human could live.

Finally, Yakubu could go no further. He was still in the midst of the jungle, but he had to sleep. All night he was pestered by mosquitoes and awakened by the sound of animals close by. Early the next morning he woke up shaking with fever. His head felt heavy and thick, still filled with the shadows of dreams. There was nothing to do but push on.

Then as the sun rose higher and the air warmed to a steamy haze, Yakubu came upon the broken twigs and snipped-off shoots of a worn deer path. He followed the path until suddenly it opened onto a well-tended plantain farm. Row after row of the tall plants stood laden with fruit. Yakubu could make no sense of this because he knew that there was no village anywhere in this jungle.

Just then, a large deer stepped lightly from between the plantain leaves. Yakubu slid back against a palm and drew back his bow. He waited breathlessly for the animal to approach. The deer peered around and tested the air with her nose three times to be sure she was alone. Then before the hunter's eyes she gracefully shed her skin and became a beautiful young woman. As she changed, she sang:

> Run to be free, be free to run,
> To breathe fresh air, and feel the sun.

The girl carefully concealed the deerskin beneath a flat stone. She picked up a basket of plantain fruit and walked to the edge of the field where the deer path resumed in the direction of the nearest town. Yakubu was not in the least afraid, for it was a common thing to hear of a deer or even a bushmouse turning into a woman. He walked confidently up to the stone and removed the deerskin. Then he placed it in the bottom of his hunting bag and awaited the return of the girl. Yakubu knew that a deer woman could not survive long in the jungle in human form.

In the evening, the girl returned with her basket filled with choice market herbs and vegetables. She looked more beautiful than ever and Yakubu knew that he must have this creature for his wife. The deer woman looked for her skin under the stone. She became angry and then frantic as she realized the danger she was in. Tears of desperation welled up in her soft brown eyes.

At this point, Yakubu rose from his hiding place and politely called to her. How, he wanted to know, did a lovely girl such as herself come to be stranded in such a terrifying jungle? Again, anger shone in the eyes of the deer woman. She sensed that it was this hunter who had taken her skin. She replied that her name was Yalwa. She had mislaid her coat and was quite helpless without it.

Yakubu boldly expressed his love for Yalwa and promised to buy her many fine coats if she would return with him and be his wife. The young woman had little choice if she was ever to recover her skin and return to her deer form, and so agreed. She silently followed Yakubu back to his village.

Yakubu lived in the same compound with Goggo, an old crone who was greatly feared by all who knew her. Goggo had powerful *juju* medicine, which she used to bring Yakubu success on his hunts. In return he shared his food with her. Goggo despised the deer woman at first sight. She could sense some kind of power in the girl and saw her as a rival who could upset her household.

At the wedding everyone celebrated, except Goggo who did everything she could to turn Yakubu against his bride. Yet Yakubu was clearly under the spell of love and would not listen to the crone. While everyone was occupied singing and dancing, Yakubu slipped away and carefully hid the deer-skin on the roof of his house.

Soon after their marriage, Yakubu's joy became complete with the twin birth of a boy and a girl to Yalwa. Yakubu rejoiced in now having a son to take hunting with him. Time passed and as soon as possible Yakubu began taking his son along on the hunting trips. He always left his daughter to be company for Yalwa and to help her clean the compound.

Goggo continued to do everything she could to make the young wife miserable. She forced Yalwa to work from morning to night whenever Yakubu was away. But for some mysterious reason, her *juju* had no effect on the deer woman. It was as if the creature had powers of her own. As Yalwa worked, she had a far-away look in her eyes. She sang sadly,

> Run to be free, be free to run,
> To breathe fresh air, and feel the sun.

One night, Goggo complained to Yakubu about how the new wife was not doing her share of the household duties. She said Yalwa was lazy and dishonest. Goggo said that she had seen Yalwa searching through the house looking for something to steal. Yakubu's eyes widened in disbelief. Then suddenly he laughed and whispered to Goggo, "I will tell you a secret. My wife is not like other women. You do not have to worry about her because she is not really even human. She is part human and part deer. I have her deer-skin and that is what she was looking for."

The astonished Goggo pretended not to believe Yakubu and suggested that he prove what he was saying. At first the hunter refused, saying that it was silly to be jealous of a deer woman. This only caused the old crone to mock him and ridicule his story. Yakubu angrily jumped up from the table. After securing Goggo's promise never to reveal his secret, he led the way up to the roof where the skin lay hidden.

For a while it appeared that the household would be peaceful. But soon enough, Goggo lost her temper. She accused Yalwa of being an animal and a witch. The proof, she shouted lay hidden on the roof! At that instant the deer woman lost all interest in the argument and hurried to retrieve her skin. She then quickly caught up her daughter and ran to the door.

The wicked Goggo stood in the doorway and tried to stop Yalwa from taking her daughter. Goggo cursed her and as the deer woman lunged, suddenly spread evil-smelling powder over the doorway. She called on all her *juju* to cause death, chanting

> Death come now,
> The time is here,
> Death come now,
> And claim this . . .

But Yalwa was too nimble. Pushing her daughter before her, she slipped by before Goggo could finish, and disap-peared into the bush.

At the time, Yakubu and his son were tracking game not too far away. A strange feeling crept over him that something was wrong. He could not tell what it was, but the feeling grew stronger until he saw two deer, one large and graceful, one still very young, trotting along the path towards him.

Yakubu notched an arrow and drew back his bow. At this distance he would not miss. He prepared to release the arrow, but something unnatural chilled him to his bones and would not let him move. Then his arm raised by itself and he let the arrow fly high overhead. It traveled back to the house and pierced the evil Goggo's heart.

The two deer seemed startled by the movement and darted like a single shadow into the bush. From a distance the deer woman's voice called out to Yakubu that she was leaving their son for him, but taking their daughter back to the jungle. Then she disappeared behind a curtain of green leaves.

For many years Yakubu searched for the plantain field, but he could never remember the way. It was as if his time with the deer woman had never been. Only his son remained to remind him that it was real.

—Based on a story by Musa Ibrahim

Akai ranar kin dillanci, ran da hajar maigari ta bata.
The day of reckoning must surely come.

T he attention of everyone in the group was riveted to Tsalla. They had all leaned forward to catch her every word. In the lamplight her eyes shone wide and round like a startled deer. Each listener could feel the hunter's chill run down his back.

Then, with a sudden sigh and a chuckle they all sat back. The street was almost deserted. Everyone had packed up and gone home to sleep. The market vendors shrugged and gathered up their wares. Some things had sold, but most would still be there next time. They were ready to go home to their families, friends, and neighbors and retell the day's stories. Each of the storytellers had a knack for grasping and remembering details of the tales they heard. But with every telling, some facts would be changed, some parts left out, others invented. Like living things, the tales would bring people together to share in the wonder of their own creation.

As Ibrahim picked up his sack of tools, he looked down the quiet street. In a courtyard in front of a nearby store, a group of people sat on chairs and benches, transfixed by a flickering light. A television set had been set up high on a shelf with an extension cord running to the store's electric power. The television was a recent addition to the village and few people could afford one. So, each evening a large group would gather to watch the one channel. It was new and it was captivating. Ibrahim saw their eyes staring blankly at the screen and could not help feeling sorry for them. The television revealed a whole world full of things and promised a better life full of happiness. But achieving it was another matter. Ibrahim preferred to rely on his own imagination and he knew that his friends could be counted on for more intriguing tales next market day.

Ibrahim's thoughts were interrupted by the headlights and loud honking horn of a lorry, rumbling down the road towards him. Its brightly painted wooden frame groaned as the truck squealed to a stop beside the vendors and the engine died.

"Where do you go?" the driver called out the window.

"Berni Nkonni! Wurno! Kware!" they answered.

"Ina zoa—I am going. I will take you. Twenty *naira,"* offered the driver.

Everyone laughed—not only because the towns were all in different directions, but because the price was so outrageously high. After much haggling, the various prices of three *naira,* one *naira,* and two *naira,* fifty *kobo* were agreed upon. These were excellent prices considering they included the transport of Musa's donkey. A wooden plank was quickly dropped from the back of the truck and the reluctant beast was half-dragged and half-pushed up the ramp.

Everyone laughed and piled into the truck, which already held several people and two goats.

Amina, Ibrahim, and Tsalla lived in town and waved good-bye to the others as the truck sputtered to life.

"*Sai an jima,* see you later and God be with you," they called as the truck roared off down the road and the taillights gradually disappeared into the night.

Glossary

Alhaji—someone who has made a pilgrimage to Mecca; a person having wealth or social status

Allah—God of Islam

Bushmouse—small, slender member of deer family, lives in forest

Calabash—dried and hollowed gourd, vessel for carrying water, sometimes carved for decoration

Cassava—crop grown throughout tropics; the starchy root is eaten similar to potato

Chop—Nigerian term for food, especially prepared food

Cowrie shells—small oval shell of mollusk commonly used for decoration, historically used by some cultures as currency

Dara—popular board and stones game similar to backgammon; outside Nigeria it is known as Mancala

Dash—Nigerian term meaning to give, usually money or possessions; dashing confirms social status; similar to tipping

Deleb palm nut—large, half shell is sometimes used as container

Falmaras—traditional sleeveless shirts often worn by traditional wrestlers

Fulani—ethnic group inhabiting Niger and northern Nigeria; traditional occupation is pastoral nomads

Gari—dry grain made by grating, fermenting, drying, and cooking cassava

Garma hoe—common short-handled hoe with flat, rounded blade used for digging

Grasscutter—large rodent similar to groundhog and rat; hunted for food in Hausaland

Groundnuts—peanuts which grow on the roots of bushes in Nigeria

Guinea corn—similar to North American corn, though smaller

Gumburai—veteran wrestler, much respected by Hausa society

Harmattan—strong winds which usually blow in December and February, create a hazy cloud of sand; considered locally to be a separate season

Jinn—magical spirit commonly believed to cause mischief or endow power

Juju—traditional medicine, often using plant or animal ingredients; can be used for good or evil

Kai—common expression of exclamation, like "Wow"

Kasuwa—outdoor marketplace; town center for trading staple goods

Kibiya awl—long, pointed iron nail used for piercing leather

Kirya wood—hot-burning hardwood favored by blacksmiths

Kobo—one hundred kobo equals one naira; ten-kobo piece called a sule is main coin of Nigerian currency

Kolanuts—traditionally given as formal gift: nuts contain caffeine and may be chewed

Koma net—also known as butterfly net, consisting of two hand-held, semi-circular nets which are brought together, trapping fish

Kunkuru stone—Hausa word for turtle; term used for weaver's stone because it is shaped like a turtle; used to keep thread running straight

Kwambala—traditional Hausa wrestling match, sometimes part of larger festival

Makodi knife—knife used by artisans for scraping and carving wood

Malam—teacher, used as "Mister," also local teacher of Islamic studies

Masaba hammer—heavy hammer used to pound heated iron into shape; the first known smelting of iron took place in the Jos plateau area of Hausaland

Matukule—song sung during the fasting period; older boys go from door to door presenting a humorous performance which is rewarded with money

Modoshi rod—blacksmith's iron tool used to burn through wood

Mosquito coil—slow-burning coil containing pesticide; smoke deters mosquitoes; ash falls from green coil onto aluminium pan

Myrrh—a gummy, fragrant substance used in traditional medicines; obtained from shrub

Naira—see Kobo above

Nim tree—hardy tree native to sub-Saharan region, it has an extensive root system to reach low water tables

Omo—laundry detergent commonly used as an all-purpose cleaner

Palm oil—reddish-brown oil made from ground palm kernels; usually imported to Hausaland from the Yoruba area of southern Nigeria

Ramadan—time of fasting and reflection for Muslims; ninth month of Islamic calendar

Riga—formal attire worn by Hausa men consisting of trousers and a loose-fitting jacket

Sabara shrub—the powdered leaves of this shrub are widely believed to have medicinal properties

Saki cloth—hand-woven black cloth with white borders

Sooya—similar to shish-ka-bob; spiced meat is seared on stick with onions and peppers

Shantali water pot—clay mixed with fine grains of sand allow small amounts of water to seep through the pot, cooling the remaining water by evaporation

Sungumi hoe—long-handled hoe used primarily for planting crops

Talking drum—famous drums of Nigeria have distinctive hourglass shape; range of tones used to imitate speech to convey messages, recite history, or sing praises to chief

Taitama anvil—heavy iron or steel bar on which blacksmith shapes metal

Tamarind tree—indigenous to West Africa, tree in which silkworms often deposit their cocoons

Tsamiya gowns—men's suits made of cloth with strands of metal, often gold, running through it, usually worn by wealthy Hausa on special occasions

Tuwo—paste used to soften leather and to stick pieces of leather together

Warki—ceremonial apron sometimes worn by wrestlers and entertainers

Zannabukar—high-brimmed, handmade fez-type cap; usual dress for Hausa men